CHARLIE

and the
Rocket Boy

CHARLIE

and the
Great Escape

Hilary McKay

Illustrated by Sam Hearn

Text copyright © Hilary McKay
Illustrations copyright © Sam Hearn

Charlie and the Great Escape was first published in Great Britain in 2007
by Scholastic Children's Books
Charlie and the Rocket Boy was first published in Great Britain in 2008 by
Scholastic Children's Books

This bind-up published in 2014 by Hodder Children's Books

The rights of Hilary McKay and Sam Hearn to be identified as the Author
and Illustrator of the Work respectively have been asserted by them in
accordance with the Copyright, Designs and Patents Act 1988

1

A Catalogue record for this book is available from the British Library

ISBN 978 1 444 91922 6

Typeset by Avon DataSet Ltd, Bidford on Avon, Warwickshire
Printed and bound by CPI Group (UK) Ltd, Croydon, CR0 4YY

Contents

Charlie and the
Rocket Boy

Best Friends

Charlie and Henry were best friends. They had been best friends for years. They had met on the Naughty Bench on their first day at pre-school when they were three years old.

Charlie had looked at Henry

and thought, I bet I could push him off.

Henry had looked at Charlie and thought, I bet I could squash him flat.

As soon as the three-years-old Charlie and Henry had thought these thoughts, they had tried them out. Sure enough, Charlie had been quite right, he could push Henry off. And about five seconds later Henry found that he was also right.

He could squash Charlie flat.

Very soon Charlie and Henry were back on the Naughty Bench again and for various reasons they stayed there for the rest of the morning.

And by home time they were best friends. Their mothers liked them being friends. It cheered them up. Secretly Charlie's mother thought Henry was

slightly worse than Charlie. Secretly
Henry's mother thought Charlie was
slightly worse than Henry. It was nice
for their mothers to think that they had
only the second naughtiest boys in pre-
school, instead of
the absolute
worst.

Charlie
and Henry
lived very
close to
each other.
They could
play at each
other's houses
whenever
they liked, and

6

when the playing turned into fighting
they could be marched home in disgrace
with no trouble at all. Very soon they
were doing almost everything together:
Easter egg hunts, haircuts, bonfire night

and shoe shopping. Also chicken pox, nits, tummy bugs and colds, because if one of them got something the other one caught it too. One summer they discovered a wasps' nest together and poked it with sticks until they were simultaneously attacked. One winter they both made traps for Father Christmas and very nearly caught him.

When Charlie and Henry started school together their mothers sighed 'At last!', hugged each other with relief, and went out to lunch to celebrate. Charlie and Henry spent the next few weeks showing their classmates how easily they could knock each other over, and how well they could squash each other flat. But still, they stayed best friends.

During lessons they sat together. At lunch time they ate together. At the end of the day they went home together.

Sometimes teachers got tired of the whisperings and pushings and grabbings that went on at Charlie and Henry's table and tried to separate them. This did not work. Charlie and Henry's behaviour did not change. It just got noisier, because they were further apart.

When Charlie and Henry were seven they moved into Mrs Holiday's class. Mrs Holiday did not try to separate them. She said, 'I might as well keep all the trouble in one place,' and gave them a special red table very close to her desk.

'Mrs Holiday colour codes the tables

9

in her room,' said Max, Charlie's big brother, who had once been in Mrs Holiday's class himself. 'Red for danger.'

'Mrs Holiday *likes* us,' said Charlie and Henry, but they asked her about their red for danger table, just in case.

'Where ever did you get such an idea?' asked Mrs Holiday.

'Max.'

'Goodness!' said Mrs Holiday. 'Oh yes, I remember Max! Very tall! School chess team and brilliant at football!'

'What colour was his table?' asked Charlie.

'I couldn't tell you,' said Mrs Holiday. 'He sat right at the back. How would you two like to be the donkey in our

10

class Christmas play?'

Charlie and Henry went suddenly
silent with joy and surprise.

'It would be perfect for you!'
continued Mrs Holiday. 'Two wonderful
starring parts! The head and the tail. I
know I can trust you not to even think
of fighting about who is which.'

Charlie and Henry, who
had been about to fight
about that very
thing,

said that of course they wouldn't.

'Very well then,' said Mrs Holiday, and so Charlie and Henry, those two best friends, were the actual donkey in the actual play and they did it very well.

'Perfect casting,' said Mrs Holiday, and gave them real carrots wrapped in silver paper for their Christmas presents, instead of boring chocolate money like everybody else.

'Told you she liked us!' said Charlie to Max.

After the Christmas play it was the end of term.

And then it was Christmas.

And then it was after Christmas, and Charlie and Henry felt like rockets that had gone up into space with a bang and a trail of stars and then come down all grey and flat and dismal to the same old planet Earth.

'Happy New Year! How soon can we take down the decorations?' asked Charlie and Henry's mums.

'Happy New Year! They will soon be back at school,' said Charlie and Henry's dads.

'Happy New Year! Cheer up! Only three hundred and fifty eight days till Christmas!' said Max.

None of this cheered Charlie and Henry up at all.

Welcome Back!

Christmas was over. The decorations were down. Now there was nothing to do but wait for Spring, and that was ages away. It was January, the coldest January anybody could remember for years.

Also it was morning on the first day of term, and Mrs Holiday, teacher of Class 3, was in the office meeting a new boy who had just arrived.

Zachary was the new boy. He had arrived very early and all alone. When Mrs Holiday first saw Zachary she thought she had never known a boy so new. He was as new as if he had

been plonked down that morning into the middle of an alien world.

Zachary had come with a letter from his last school.

Zachary likes to talk about his family, it said. But often questions upset him, because he does not

know the answers.

Mrs Holiday could understand that. She did not ask questions. She just smiled and led him along the corridors to her class.

'We have never had a Zachary before,' she told him as they walked. 'You will be our first.'

'Maybe there are no more Zacharys,' said Zachary. 'Could be that I am the only one.'

'That makes us very lucky then, doesn't it?' said Mrs Holiday.

Zachary managed to smile a little.

'Do you know what I say to myself at the start of term?' asked Mrs Holiday. 'I say, Courage!'

'Courage?'

'That's right. It helps. And if somebody says it to me, that helps, too!'

'Courage, Mrs Holiday!' said Zachary.

'Courage, Zachary!' said Mrs Holiday, leading him into the empty classroom. 'Now, let me find a home for you!'

She looked around the classroom thoughtfully. Not at the back, where the brainy ones sat, that was too far away. Not with the boys whose favourite thing was football because Zachary from America would not know about English football. Not on the blue table of never-stop-talkers where Zachary would never get a chance to speak. Not on the yellow table of perfect-school-uniform,

huge-stuffed-pencil case people either.
Zachary had arrived with nothing at all.

'Here you are, Zachary!' she decided
at last and pulled out a chair for him.
'Quite close to me, and a lovely view of
the guinea pig!'

So Zachary sat down and looked
quietly at the guinea pig and the guinea
pig looked quietly back at Zachary and
the room was perfectly silent, waiting
for the day to begin. Meanwhile,
Charlie and Henry were on their way
to school. Also they were in the middle
of a quarrel about Henry's new remote
control car (which was lost somewhere
at Charlie's house) and Charlie's new
electric guitar (which Henry had retuned
the day before with terrible string-

snapping results).

Charlie and Henry had spent most of the Christmas holiday quarrelling, starting the day after Christmas when the Curly Wurly from Charlie's Selection Box and the Jelly Santa from Henry's stocking had mysteriously gone missing.

This morning Charlie and Henry were especially grumpy. They had not felt like

getting up in the dark and putting on
school uniform and eating chilly cereal
and plodding up the road in the cold.

WELCOME BACK!

read a sign over the school front door.

'I wish I was still in bed!' grumbled
Charlie, shrugging off his school bag in
the cloakroom and accidentally hitting

Henry in the eye.

'*I* wish you were still in bed!' said
Henry crossly, pushing him out of the
way.

They stamped into the classroom not
pleased with the world, and there was
Zachary, sitting at their table.

Charlie and Henry were shocked. In
an instant they forgot the Jelly Santa

and the Curly Wurly. The remains of
the electric guitar and the lost remote
control car (gone forever down the back
of Charlie's mum's washing machine)
suddenly did not matter. Instantly they
were best friends again, the sort of
friends who did not want anybody else.
And each of them knew, without saying
a word, that of all the people they did
not want, they did not want this one
most of all. This boy with the round
blue eyes and round yellow curls and
round pink face and no school uniform.

'Why haven't you got school
uniform?' hissed Henry to Zachary, the
moment he sat down.

'Because I'm not staying,' said
Zachary. 'I'm only here for a while.'

'Just today?' asked Charlie hopefully.

'More than that.'

'Just this week then?'

'No, more than that.'

'*How* long then?' demanded Charlie, forgetting to whisper, and Mrs Holiday, who had been filling in the register, said, 'Charlie!' and glared at him.

Mrs Holiday had a glare like a weapon. Charlie always hated it when she aimed it at him. He could feel exactly where her eyes were pointing. They felt like two icy fingers on the back of his neck. Wriggling made no difference. So Charlie shut up.

'I am trying to fill in the register,' said Mrs Holiday, removing the icy fingers from Charlie for a moment and flicking them across to the top of Henry's head. 'And I would like a little hush.'

Charlie rubbed the back of his neck, and Henry rubbed the top of his head, and they looked across at Zachary to see if he was sorry about getting them into all this trouble. The guinea pig came over to the bars of the cage to look as well. Zachary looked back at all three of them and smiled. A little smile for Charlie and Henry, and then a much bigger one for the guinea pig.

Zachary didn't seem to understand there was any trouble.

He didn't look sorry at all.

Zachary

After she had finished the register Mrs Holiday introduced Zachary to the class. She said, 'Zachary has come all the way from America to be with us for a while. I hope you will all be very good friends. Would you like to tell us a little bit about yourself, Zachary?'

For a moment it looked like Zachary

wouldn't. He gazed around the class as if there was nothing he could tell them that they could possibly understand. But then he seemed to change his mind, and he stood up.

He said, 'My name is Zachary but most folks call me Zack. I am seven going on eight. I have come a long way. My dad is an astronaut on his way to a star.

'It will take him two n'half years to get there, and two n'half to get back so I shall be more than

27

thirteen when I see him again.'

Then he sat down.

There was moment of stunned silence, and then Class 3 erupted. They had never heard such a ridiculous story! They had never heard such awful showing off! Twenty-six hands shot up as high as they could reach. Several people jumped up, so as to get their hands even higher. The noise was immense. It sounded like the classroom was falling apart.

'QUIET, EVERYONE!' said Mrs Holiday in her loudest voice. 'HENRY! PICK UP YOUR CHAIR! CHARLIE STOP SHOUTING! HANDS DOWN ALL OF YOU! Now, Zachary!'

'Yes ma'am?' said Zachary politely.

'Thank you for talking to us. It is not easy to stand up like that and talk to so many people. You did very well indeed. Charlie, stop waving your hand about!'

Charlie stopped waving his hand

about because Mrs Holiday was looking so fierce. She would not let anyone ask a single question about Zachary's father. She would not let anyone say that what he had told them could not possibly be true. She acted like she believed every word. Only Charlie was allowed to speak, and only after he had promised he really had something sensible to say.

When Charlie was excited or bothered about something his voice went squeaky. It was squeaky now as he said,

'If Zack is seven going on eight and it takes two'n'half years to get to the star and two'n'half to get back then that is only five years his dad will be gone. So Zack will be twelve when he gets home, not more than thirteen like he said.'

'Good Heavens, Charlie!' said Mrs Holiday, looking truly astonished. 'I believe that is the first time I have ever heard you do maths on purpose! *And* you got it *right*! Zachary? Please can you explain to Charlie?'

Zachary stood up again, as if he had been asked to explain to the whole class, not just Charlie.

He said, 'He's got stuff to do when he gets there. He's not going to go all that way and take all that time and then just turn right round and come back. He's got to look around and do stuff.'

Mrs Holiday was giving her class a look which said as plainly as speaking, Move one finger, speak one word, and you are all in at break time!

'He's got seeds to plant,' said Zachary.

'*On a star*?!' exploded Henry, before he could stop himself.

'Henry, apologize to Zachary or leave the room!' ordered Mrs Holiday.

''Pologize, Zachary,' muttered Henry furiously.

'Seeds to plant,' repeated Zachary, as if nothing at all had happened to interrupt him. 'And then, I suppose he'll have to hang around and wait and see if they come up. That'll take time. So, I'm going to be thirteen when he gets back,' Zachary paused. 'I guess,' he said, and sighed.

Mrs Holiday seemed to want to change the subject. She said it had been very interesting to hear about Zachary's father, and now they would do maths.

They were doing charts and graphs, and she said they would make a chart called a bar chart showing everyone's pets. Very quickly she began to write up on the board all the sorts of pets people had. She made everyone help.

They counted five dogs, eleven cats, two rabbits, two hamsters, five guinea pigs, one cockatoo and nineteen goldfish and then Zachary put up his hand and said, 'Four horses.' Charlie and Henry jumped up so fast they banged their heads together.

'Four horses?' asked Mrs Holiday.

'I have four horses,' said Zachary.

Mrs Holiday wrote FOUR HORSES at the bottom of her list on the board and took no notice of Henry and Charlie.

'Anything else?' she asked.

'No, ma'am,' said Zachary.

The four horses went on to the chart with all the rest of the animals.

Mrs Holiday would not let anyone say that nobody has four horses.

Once the four horses were down on the list Zachary took no more notice of the maths lesson. He sat through it as if it was something going on far, far away from him. As if he was peacefully watching it through a telescope, slightly interested and slightly sleepy.

It was not the same for the rest of Class 3. To them it seemed the longest lesson ever, and they themselves felt like balloons blown up too hard and about to explode. Even Charlie (newly discovered mathematical genius) could hardly bear it.

But at last it was break.

The whole class rushed out into the playground and surrounded Zachary.

They had decided what they thought about him, with his four horses, and his dad on a two and a half year long journey to a star. They sang,

'Liar, liar! Pants on fire!

LIAR, LIAR! PANTS ON FIRE!'

Zachary stood and looked at them with his hands in his pockets and a little

35

frown on his forehead, and his round
blue eyes even rounder than ever.

Liar, Liar! Pants on Fire!

'**D**isgraceful!' exclaimed Mrs Holiday, appearing from nowhere and freezing them all into silence with one terrible look.

'Inside, all of you! Zachary, wait here! Charlie and Henry, what do you think you are doing?'

Charlie and Henry had not joined in the singing of 'Liar, liar! Pants on fire!'

with everyone else. This was because in the mad rush to get out of the classroom Charlie had tripped over his feet and landed sprawled on the ground. While he was rolling around saying, 'Oh, oh, nobody cares!' Henry had seen the wonderful chance to sit on his friend's stomach and tie the laces of his two shoes together in a big hard knot.

Charlie and Henry had been too busy huffing and kicking and wrestling to sing. Therefore, when Mrs Holiday stormed outside to her class they escaped the worst of her anger. They were told to stop being silly and put their shoes on properly, and show Zachary around the playground a little and make him feel at home.

Charlie and Henry showed Zachary the football field, the Friendship Bench ('You're supposed to sit on it if you haven't any friends,' explained Henry, and Zachary obligingly sat down), the old nest that the swallows had built, the outside tap by the caretaker's room, and the teachers' car park.

'Once when it was winter like this, the outside tap dripped,' said Charlie, 'and the water made a great puddle in that dip in the middle of the teachers' car park and it all froze solid and we made slides. But they put salt on the slides and fixed the tap.'

Zachary said, 'At home there is a

whole lake that freezes solid and we go skating and sliding in the moonlight and wolves come out of the trees and sit round the edge watching, but it's perfectly safe because they can't run on ice. Having four legs means they slide four ways at once and get nowhere. Of course, they won't come near the bonfires.'

Neither Charlie nor Henry had ever been to America, but suddenly they saw in their minds a picture of a frozen lake and moonlight and firelight and shadowy trees and wolves. They saw it so clearly they were stunned, and for ever afterwards, when Charlie and Henry heard the word 'America', that was the thing they thought of first.

Now they stared at Zachary and their mouths fell open and stayed that way.

That was why they did not say, 'Liar, liar! Pants on fire!'

'It is a pity they fixed that dripping tap,' continued Zachary, seeming to be talking as much to himself as Charlie and Henry. 'I really like skating. Especially at night. On clear frosty nights you can see my father's rocket heading towards his star. I miss my dad.

And my mom. She's down in Florida right now. Disneyland.'

Just then the bell went and they had to hurry back inside where Mrs Holiday was being so frighteningly polite nobody dared hardly speak for the whole of the rest of the day.

This meant that Henry had no chance of informing Zachary of something he knew for absolutely certain until the end of school.

'Disneyland,' said Henry, 'is in France! Paris! I've been there! You ask anyone in this class if you don't believe me!'

But Zachary did not ask anyone. He just gazed solemnly at Henry with his round blue eyes, shook his head and said, 'I think you are a little mixed up, Charlie.'

And then he walked away, leaving Henry to walk home with Charlie chattering with indignation.

'He called me Charlie!' said Henry. 'Do I look like you?'

'NO!' said Charlie. 'DEFINITELY NOT! You're titchy! You've got weird hair! You've got yoghurt down your front! You wear girls' white socks ...'

'You wear a vest,' said Henry, which silenced Charlie. 'Anyway we're talking about Zachary. Do you know what he said when I told him where Disneyland was? He said I was mixed up! I've *been* there, Charlie!'

'Yes you have,' agreed Charlie,

adding very quietly to himself, 'You showed off about it for weeks.'

'I brought you back that giant lolly that pulled your tooth out.'

'I know.'

'I don't suppose you've got it any more? Not even the wrapper?'

'Why would I have kept the wrapper?'

'As a souvenir of me going to Disneyland. *Disneyland, Paris*! We could have shown it to Zachary for proof.'

MUNCH

CRUNCH

'He wouldn't have taken any notice,' said Charlie.

'He doesn't take any notice of anything, hardly.'

Henry admitted that this was true.

'What I think about Zachary,' said Henry, 'is that saying, "Liar, liar! Pants on fire!" to him is a complete waste of time.'

'What I think about Zachary,' said Charlie, 'is that listening to him is making my brain feel weird. Like it's spinning round and round inside my head.'

Henry agreed with that.

'Wolves!' said Charlie.

'I know,' said Henry. 'Four horses!'

'I know,' said Charlie.

'And that rocket! Did you understand any of that?'

'I understood the maths, Henry,' said Charlie smugly. 'Do you want me to explain?'

'Not right now,' said Henry.

Then they plodded on in silence for a while, until Charlie said suddenly, 'We didn't say, "Liar, liar! Pants on fire!"'

'No.'

'But it can't be true, all that stuff he told us?'

'No,' said Henry. 'Of course it can't.'

'Why not?'

'Charlie,' said Henry impatiently, 'Did it *sound* true?'

'No,' admitted Charlie. 'But ...'

'But what?'

'Wouldn't it be good if it was?'

Frost and Ice

Charlie and Henry told their mothers about Zachary.

'Poor little boy!' said Henry's mother.

'Poor!' repeated Henry to Charlie afterwards. 'My mum's bonkers! He's got four horses! He's not poor!'

'I should think only millionaires have four horses,' agreed Charlie.

'Billionaires!'

'Trillionaires!'

'I've never heard of one of those,' said Henry, and Charlie, who was not really sure that he had either, changed the subject by saying, 'My mum said to ask him to tea.'

'Ask Zachary to tea,' said Charlie's mother. 'I should like to meet him.'

'Why?'

'To be friendly, of course!'

'If I ask him to tea to be friendly, then he will think he is my friend.'

'Good.'

'I could ask Henry to tea, if you want to have somebody round,' suggested Charlie.

'No thank you, Charlie! That is not

what I meant.'

'I don't see why you wouldn't like to meet Henry just as much as Zachary.'

'I have *met* Henry,' said Charlie's mother, not very patiently, 'I have met him at least once nearly every day for the last four and a half years. I have patched up his knees and got mud out of his hair. I forgave him for trying to drown you that time in the paddling pool. I carted him off to hospital the day he told me he couldn't

move his
legs for a
practice
April Fools'. I
have cooked
him a
mountain of
dinners and
teas and lunches and
suppers. I know him very well indeed
and I WOULD LIKE A CHANGE!'

'Oh.'

'So ask Zachary to tea AND THAT'S
AN ORDER!'

'My mum said I've got to ask you to
tea,' said Charlie to Zachary.

'Why?' asked Zachary.

'Because she's bored with Henry.'

'*Bored with ME?*' repeated Henry, amazed and disbelieving. 'Was she joking?'

'No.'

'I bet she was,' said Henry. 'Bored with me! Ha!'

'She wasn't joking at all,' said Charlie. 'She was in a very bad mood. She said she wanted a change from you and when I argued she said "Ask Zachary to tea AND THAT'S AN ORDER!"'

Zachary looked all round the room, at the windows and the doors and the guinea pig cage and under the table. Under the table he seemed to find an answer.

'Anyhow,' he said. 'I don't like tea.'

So that was the end of that.

Over the next few days the frost and ice grew worse. Mrs Holiday began wearing new fur boots for playground duty. 'They make her legs look like

lovely sheeps' bottoms,' remarked one of the girls. Zachary learnt to tell the difference between Henry and Charlie. Nothing else changed.

Zachary's tales grew more and more unbelievable. He told anyone who would listen about the boiling geysers he had seen ('like mini volcanoes of hot mud,' said Zachary), the quad bike he owned back home in America, the tooth he had swallowed during silent reading,

and his grandmother in England, who he said was a witch.

Charlie's brain spun round and round inside his head and he did not know what to think.

Henry did. Henry had started saying, 'Liar, liar! Pants on fire!' to each new story, even though he said before that it was a complete waste of time.

'Somebody has to tell him what we think,' said Henry primly. Charlie said it as well sometimes, but he did not say it comfortably because he had actually seen Zachary swallow the tooth.

The weather continued to be icy cold with bright starry nights. Zachary spent a lot of his break times gazing at the dip in the middle of the teachers' car park, and at the outside tap that did not leak any more. Charlie and Henry used to watch him. They knew he was thinking of his frozen lake where the wolves came out of the trees, and the bonfires burned, and the nights were so clear that you could see a rocket heading for a star two and a half years away.

Then one night Charlie went with his parents to meet his big brother Max from a friend's house. They walked, because Charlie's parents said that would be quicker than defrosting the car. Max's friend lived on the road that went past the school, and on the way home Max and Charlie lagged behind their parents and Charlie told him for

the first time the story about Zachary's
father and the rocket.

Max looked up at the sky and said, 'I
wonder which star.'

This gave Charlie a creepy feeling
down his back, which became ten times

more creepy when they passed the school. Because in the shadowy playground he was sure he saw a little figure slip silently round a corner.

There was a sort of glow around the little figure's head, which Charlie guessed was how yellow curls looked by starlight.

'Did you see anyone?' he asked Max. 'Where?'

'In the playground, sort of hiding.'

'Mrs Holiday, waiting to pounce?' asked Max grinning, and did a very good impression of Mrs Holiday pouncing on Charlie.

'Much smaller than Mrs Holiday,' said Charlie, pushing him away.

'Didn't see anyone,' said Max, 'but

we can go back and look if you like.'

'No!' exclaimed Charlie in sudden alarm, and to prevent Max doing such a thing added, 'Race you to Mum and Dad!' and skidded away up the road before Max could disagree.

Max tore after him, and between them they nearly swept their mother off her feet, and then they ran on down the road together, dodging the shadows under the darkest hedges, leaping the blackness of silent open gates, collapsing with thumping hearts at each friendly lamp post.

The more they ran, the better Charlie felt. It was delicious to be frightened and running in the night if you had your big brother beside you, your mum and dad not far behind, and home just round the corner with the lights on and Suzy the cat watching out from the windowsill. He forgot the little figure that he had half seen in the playground.

But when the house was quiet and he was safe in bed for the night he remembered and, despite his quilt,

and his extra fleecy blanket, and his dinosaur hot water bottle and his winter pyjamas, the memory made him shiver.

Had that been Zachary in the playground? He wished now that he and Max had gone back to see.

But we didn't, thought Charlie. We ran home.

Then he remembered Zachary saying, that first unfriendly day, 'I have come a long way.'

You cannot run home to America, thought Charlie. You cannot run home to a star.

Poor Zachary, thought Charlie.

It was the first time ever he had thought that thought.

Terrible Trouble

The next day there was terrible trouble at school. Overnight, the car park had become a black sheet of ice. The Head Teacher's car skidded and smashed into the caretaker's room with a horrible scrunching sound. The caretaker had rushed outside to see what was happening and had fallen and broken his leg. Then an ambulance

arrived and drove the caretaker to
hospital, and after that a breakdown
truck came to school and took the Head
Teacher's car away.

Mrs Holiday also had trouble on
the car park ice. She slipped down so
hard in her sheeps' bottom boots that
she had a great black bruise all up one
arm, and another on the side of her
head that made one eye swell up. But
she would not allow herself to be taken

away like the caretaker and the Head Teacher's car. She came into class and she said, 'The school car park is totally out of bounds. That outside tap leaked so much that the whole area is one huge patch of ice. Poor Mrs Smith's car is wrecked and later on we will all make Get Well Cards for the caretaker, who has broken his leg.'

Then she shot icy cold glares all around the room from her one good eye.

Charlie felt sick. He thought he was going to have to tell on Zachary, and he did not want to. He thought of himself and Max racing past to their parents and their warm safe home, and he remembered the loneliness he had glimpsed in the playground the night before. He did not understand Zachary any more than he had the first day they met, but suddenly he was on his side, and he did not know what to do.

Zachary knew what to do.

Zachary stood up and said, 'It was me. I am very sorry. I turned on the tap last night. I wanted to make a frozen lake.'

Mrs Holiday looked at Zachary as if she loved him and she said, 'That was a very brave and honest thing to say, Zachary. Very brave and very honest. I am proud of you.'

Then Henry was so ashamed that he had ever sung 'Liar, liar! Pants on fire!' to Zachary that he put his head down on the table and started to cry.

Nobody else said a word, not even Mrs Holiday, until Charlie called out, in his squeakiest voice, 'I am proud of him too!' and he put one arm round Henry, and the other round Zachary.

'I wish he was stopping for always, not just for a while,' said Charlie.

The Rocket and the Star

Charlie's wish did not come true. Just when they got used to him, Zachary said, 'I've got to go.'

'WHAT?!' shouted Charlie and Henry.

If Charlie and Henry were shocked when Zachary came they were absolutely outraged when he said he had to go.

'You can't!' they said. 'You've only just got here! Who says you've got to? What do you mean, go?'

'Back,' explained Zachary.

'Back where?'

'Just back,' said Zachary, who never seemed to know where he was, except that it was not home. 'Soon.'

'Soon?' asked Charlie. 'When is soon?'

'Saturday.'

'Saturday! It's Tuesday now!'

'We've hardly got to know him!' complained Charlie to Max.

'You didn't want to know him.'

'He never even came to tea.'

'Whose fault was that?'

'There's loads he never told us!'

'Would you have believed him if he

68

had?' Recently Max had somehow heard about the singing, 'Liar, liar! Pants on Fire!' He had told Charlie what he thought of that.

'But there isn't time for anything!' Charlie complained.

'There was time,' said unsympathetic Max. 'You were horrible, all of you! A gang of little rotters, thinking you knew everything! You don't look further than the ends of your stuck up noses!'

'Neither do you,' growled Charlie, but really he knew that it was not true. Max had not said 'Liar!' Max had said, 'I wonder which star.'

'What can I do?' wailed Charlie. 'How can we make it up?'

'Think,' said Max.

Charlie thought. He chewed his knuckles and thought. He pulled his hair and thought. He pounded his head into his pillow and thought and thought and at last he had an idea.

'But it might not be a good one,' he said to Henry. 'How can I tell?'

'Ask Mrs Holiday,' said Henry.

'It might be good,' said Mrs Holiday,

when she heard it. 'Let me talk to Zachary.'

'Yes.'

'And his grandmother.'

'All right.'

'And check the weather forecast.'

'I forgot about that.'

'And we'd have to send letters home.'

'All those things,' said Charlie, and sighed.

'I will do them as fast as I can,' said Mrs Holiday, but all the same it was Thursday before she could tell him, 'It was a good idea!'

On Friday afternoon Mrs Holiday's class stayed on after school. They had biscuits and blackcurrant juice and a

71

chocolate cake delivered by Zachary's grandmother (who said very little and went away early and certainly looked like a witch). After that they played games until the windows grew black and outside it was proper dark night.

Then at last Mrs Holiday said it was time to get ready and they all wrapped up warm and went out into the playground, and Zachary pointed to where they should look.

Everyone saw quite plainly the rocket and the star.

Charlie and the
Great Escape

Going

Charlie had a very sad hard life. He had a terrible family who did not appreciate him.

Charlie was seven years old and he lived with his brother Max, who was eleven years old, and his

father and mother, who were ancient.

'They like Max best,' Charlie told his best friend Henry.

It was a sunny afternoon in the summer holidays. Charlie was spending it in Henry's garden, which was just down the road from his own. He was having a good grumble.

'They like Max *much* better than me! They laugh at *his* jokes ...'

'Don't they laugh at yours?'

'No,' said Charlie. 'They say stuff like, "Charlie, that is not the sort of thing anyone wants to hear about at the dinner table". And they hate my mouth-organ playing. My dad shouts,

"Somewhere else, please Charlie!" the second I begin.'

'My mum *asks* me to play my recorder,' remarked Henry smugly.

'*My* mum,' said Charlie, 'groans when I come into a room. And says, "Shoes off, Charlie, before you take another step!" And she goes on and on about interrupting people talking. How can I not interrupt when she talks all the time? I have to yell to make her take any notice of me.'

'I've heard you,' agreed Henry. 'If your front door's open we can hear you right down the road.'

'And the fuss she makes if I come home in the wrong clothes if I've accidentally put on someone else's after PE! Or about lost socks! My mum's got a thing about socks. Every time I come home without them she goes mad!'

'What does it matter about losing socks?' asked Henry in astonishment. 'Everyone has socks! I have thousands!'

'I have three,' said Charlie.

'Borrow Max's.'

'Oh ha ha ha,' said Charlie bitterly. 'As if that could ever happen! *None* of my family share *anything* with me.'

'*I* share with you,' said Henry. 'At least you've got *me*.'

'S'pose,' said Charlie ungratefully.  'And when you're grown up you can run away from your terrible family!'

'I could run away now,' said Charlie. 'That would show them! Then they'd be sorry!'

'They might be *pleased*,' remarked Henry. 'Then what?'

Instead of answering that unsympathetic question, Charlie rugby-tackled Henry's knees. They fell together in a scuffling heap on top of Henry's mother's washing basket, which was full of clean wet washing waiting for a space on the line. Henry grabbed a T-shirt and washed Charlie's face with it. Charlie stuffed a pair of damp pants down Henry's neck. For the next few minutes they whacked each other with bunches of wet socks. After that Charlie got Henry flat on his back and very cleverly managed to force Henry's mother's nightdress over his head, proving he had won. Henry pulled it off and it ripped, and then both their mothers rushed out into the garden and caught them.

Henry's mother said it did not matter a bit.

Charlie's mother said it mattered very much indeed and she marched Charlie home straight away, instead of letting him stay for tea-and-*The-Simpsons* as she had previously agreed he could do.

'This is the sort of thing,' called Charlie over his shoulder to Henry as he was led away, 'that happens to me *all the time*!'

Going

That was on Wednesday. On Thursday morning Charlie's sad hard life got suddenly sadder and harder. Max was out in the park with a football, his ancient dad was messing about at work with his friends, his ancient mother was messing about at home with the cat, but Charlie was jailed in his bedroom.

The day had hardly begun. Charlie had padded downstairs to the empty kitchen, loaded the toaster and been sent back to his room again. Before his toast had even popped up. Simply because, while waiting for his toast, he had prized the free CD off the front of the cereal packet and tried it out in the new computer that his father had just brought home from work.

The computer made grating sounds and flashed a hundred exciting screens and Charlie's mother came in and yelled, 'Back upstairs you go before I completely lose my temper!'

As if she had not completely lost it already.

'What about my toast?' asked Charlie.

'Bother your toast!' shouted Charlie's mother, who grabbed it out of the toaster, flung it into the bin and started trying to get the cereal box disc out of the computer.

'Use a spoon,' advised Charlie.

'WHAT?'

'I used a spoon to get it in.'

'Charlie,' said Charlie's mother in

86

 an awful voice.
'Vanish!'
At first
(except for
missing his
toast) Charlie
did not mind too much. His PlayStation
was in his bedroom, and so was Max's
new racing-car game. But it was not
long before his mother heard the roaring
of car engines and the screech of brakes
and stamped upstairs and switched it
all off. She seemed to think that Charlie
should not be having fun.

For a little while Charlie thought he
would leave it all unplugged for ever
and that would show how sad and hard
his life was.

Then he thought he would plug it all
back in again, and that would show his
mum.

And then he remembered the
conversation in Henry's garden the day
before, and he thought he would run
away, and that would show everyone.

This seemed the best idea of all, and
so he began to pack.

In Max's rucksack he packed his

bear, his money box, his
photograph album of
pictures of himself, and a
large bag of stones that
he had collected on the beach in case
they were valuable. Also he
took a trick fly-in-an-ice-
cube, a squirting calculator,

some plastic dog poo, a half-
used packet of itching powder,
his last two remaining foaming blood
sugar lumps, two socks and one glow-
in-the-dark skeleton T-shirt.
As a souvenir of his ancient
father he took his torch, and
as a souvenir of Max he
took his stick of seaside
rock, but he did not bother
taking a souvenir of his
mother because she did not own any
good stuff.

When he had filled the rucksack he
crept on to the landing and collected
two big holdalls from the little cupboard
there. In one of them he put his
PlayStation, and in the other he put the

portable TV that went with it. In the
past Charlie had moaned about this TV,
since it was, as Max once remarked, the
smallest and cheapest that money could
buy. Now he was thankful that it was
not any bigger. Even as it was, with the
rucksack on his back, the PlayStation
holdall across one shoulder, and the TV
across the other, he could hardly stand
up.

Still, he managed, and after a bit
of practice walking up and down his
bedroom it got easier. Everything was
fastened to him, so he could not actually
drop anything, as long as he stayed
upright.

Then Charlie, holding tight to the
banister, went very slowly down the
stairs, very slowly through the kitchen,

and very slowly out of the door.

Outside the door he stood on the path and thought. It seemed all wrong that he was running away without anyone noticing. So very slowly he went back into the house again.

'I'm running away!' he shouted, and then he slammed the door so hard that the last sound he heard from his home was the crack of breaking glass.

Charlie did not look back. He stumped up the garden path and turned on to the street. There he found that a sunny morning in the

school holidays was the worst time possible to run away. There were people everywhere. The first two he met were Lulu, the girl next door, and her best friend Mellie. They were whizzing about on Rollerblades.

'Get out of the way *quick*, Charlie!' they shouted, rushing towards him at a hundred miles an hour.

Charlie could not do anything quick, but his bags saved him from being knocked flat. The heaviness of them rooted him to the ground like a tree stump and the girls bounced off, rubbing their elbows and exclaiming at the hardness of Charlie's corners.

'Where are you going?' they asked. 'Aren't you hot, carrying all that?

You need a wheelbarrow! You need a
lorry! You've gone all red! What *are* you
doing?'

'I'm running away,' said Charlie.

'Running!' they repeated.

'Yes, running,' said Charlie solidly,
and he put his head down and continued
his tortoise-like progress for about
another ten seconds when he collided
with Henry's mother.

'Ouch!' she said. 'Charlie! Where *are*
you going with all those bags?'

'I'm run –' began Charlie, and then caught sight of the girls, listening and clutching each other and giggling. 'I'm walking ... I'm just walking ... you know ...'

'Yes?' asked Henry's mother.

'I'm just walking away,' said Charlie and he walked away to show her what he meant and with every step he felt her staring eyes on his breaking back.

It is totally-end-of-the-world Not Fair! grumbled Charlie to himself. I can't even run away in peace!

'Morning, Max!' said the postman, right in front of him.

'I'm not Max,' growled Charlie crossly, and he thought, What unbelievable bad luck! The postman now!

'You're not Max?'

'No,' said Charlie, swaying under his bags.

'Well, let's get this right,' said the postman, as if Charlie had all the time in the world to chat. 'There's that Henry, number sixty? Right?'

'I s'pose,' groaned Charlie, shrugging his aching shoulders.

'That big dog at number sixty-two, which I don't stop at because he'll have the door down one of these days.'

Charlie sighed.

'Madam on wheels over there at number sixty-four?'

Charlie's bags seemed to grow heavier every moment. He shuffled and swayed and longed for the postman to shut up. When he could bear the strain no longer he went and leaned on number sixty-two's fence. The fence leaned too, further and further backwards under his weight. Inside the house a dog went mad.

'... and so I thought you must be Max,' continued the postman, taking no notice of any of this. 'Max who gets postcards from America at number sixty-six ...'

Charlie and the fence were now in a perilous position, halfway between upright and flat on the ground.

'Unless,' continued the postman, 'you *also* live at number sixty-six *but* you don't get post. Could that be you?'

Charlie nodded, which was a big

mistake. The fence collapsed and Charlie buckled at the knees and went down with it. Inside the house the dog ripped down a curtain. Then the front door flew open, the dog charged out and the postman and the lady at number sixty-two started shouting at each other.

Charlie crawled hurriedly away, dragged himself upright at the nearby lamp post and looked around. He felt

he needed somewhere to hide, and the only place he could think of was back at his own house, the secret wild patch between the shed and the hedge where he had hidden from trouble all his life.

Two minutes later that was where he was. It felt wonderful. It felt like the far side of the world. It felt like, if you had to run away, then this was the perfect place to go.

This is where I am going to stay, thought Charlie happily.

Gone

For a long time Charlie did nothing but lie on his back and suck Max's stick of rock and listen to the faraway sounds of cars and doors and Lulu and Mellie falling over. And then he heard someone come into the garden and knock on the back door. It was Henry's knock, Charlie knew it at once, so when the door opened he listened very hard indeed.

'Did you know your door glass was cracked?' he heard Henry ask.

'Yes, thank you, Henry,' said Charlie's mother, perfectly calmly. 'Charlie did it.'

'Oh,' said Henry. 'Is he grounded then? Or is he playing?'

'I am sorry, Henry,' said Charlie's mother, 'but he isn't grounded or playing. He has run away.'

'He said he might,' said Henry, sounding not a bit surprised. 'Where's he gone to, then?'

'Goodness knows,' said Charlie's

mother. 'To sea, perhaps. Or to look for treasure. Somewhere like that, I suppose. I am afraid I shall have to go now, Henry. I am trying to fix the computer that he wrecked this morning with a disc from a cereal packet which I told him not to put in. It is making a terrible grinding sound and all the text is in Japanese and it is not even our computer. Charlie's father borrowed it from work ...'

Her voice trailed away. Charlie heard the door close and then a little scratchy noise that he knew was Henry's interested fingers exploring the crack in the glass. Very carefully he stuck his head out into the open and hissed, 'Henry!'

Henry gave a great terrified jump.

'I'm here! Behind you!'

'Oh!' exclaimed Henry. 'Oh! It's you! I thought you'd run away!'

'I have. To here behind the shed. Come and look!'

'I've seen behind your shed millions of times,' grumbled Henry, but he crawled round after Charlie anyway, and looked again.

'It's just the same,' he said. 'Not very nice.'

'I think it's brilliant. No one will ever know I'm here.'

'They will if they look behind the shed,' said Henry.

'Yes, but they *won't* look behind the shed,' replied Charlie. 'Dad's too big.

Mum's scared of spiders. And Max thinks he's much too important. I'm going to make it all comfy and stay here until they're sorry.'

'I think your mum's sorry already,' said Henry. 'She's sorry you wrecked that computer, anyway.'

'That's not the sort of sorry I meant,' said Charlie. 'Now, go and ask my mum if you can play in our garden.'

'Why?'

'Because,' said Charlie, 'then you will be useful.'

Charlie's mother seemed rather surprised to see Henry at the door again. However, she said he could play in the garden if he wanted to, and she hoped he would not be bored.

'I am used to being bored,' said Henry. 'My family are very boring people.'

'Well, just as you please,' said Charlie's mother. 'I will be in the front room cleaning lemonade-bottle rocket fuel off the carpet. And walls. Do you know how to make a lemonade-bottle rocket, Henry?'

'Oh yes,' said Henry. 'You partly fill it with water and pump it up with a bike pump. We did it at school in science.'

'Outside or inside?' asked Charlie's mother.

'Outside.'

'Last night Charlie discovered that it works just as well inside,' said Charlie's mother. 'And you don't need water.

Orange juice is just as good.'

'Is the computer fixed?'

'No. It has Frozen. Oh, Henry, you might dump this on the bird table for me, as you go past. It is nearly lunch time.'

She led him into the kitchen and handed him a large picnic plate. Henry stared at it in astonishment.

'Do you always feed the birds like this at lunch time?' he asked.

'I do since Charlie ran away,' said Charlie's mother, and shooed him back into the garden.

Since Charlie had finished Max's stick of rock, starving to death had been one of his biggest worries.

'What is it?' he asked, popping out as soon as his mother had gone.

'Cheese sandwiches, apple pies, crisps and tomatoes,' said Henry, heading for the bird table.

'Don't dump
it on there!
Bring it here!
I'm starving.'

'You can't

107

eat bird food. You'll drop down dead!'

Charlie did not agree, and after a few minutes of watching him gobble, Henry decided he might be right, and joined in before everything disappeared.

Between bites, Charlie gave orders.

'Carpet,' he said. 'I shall need a carpet. And a bed. And something to put my drink of water on in the night. And somewhere for my TV and PlayStation and an axe or a very sharp knife. I need to cut a hole in the shed.'

'Why do you need to cut a hole in the shed?' demanded Henry.

'You'll see,' said Charlie. 'Carpet first! What about that Thomas the Tank Engine rug in your bedroom? You're much too old for Thomas! I've thought so for ages.'

'You've wanted it for ages, you mean,' said Henry, scooping up the last of the crisps. 'But I'll fetch it if you like. I'll go now and eat my apple pie on the way. And that sandwich if you don't want it …'

Charlie passed it over, and Henry set off. He was back very soon with the rug

rolled up under one arm. With his other hand he dragged along his beanbag. This was a horrible thing shaped like a legless purple horse. It had been passed on to Henry by his cousin Lily, and he had been trying to get rid of it for months.

'It'll do for a bed if you curl up,' he said proudly. 'And I brought you a tin-opener because I couldn't find an axe or a very sharp knife. Here you are. Now don't wake me up for a bit!'

He curled up on the beanbag, tucked himself up with the Thomas rug and did some pretend snoring.

Charlie, who had already started hacking at the base of the shed with the tin-opener, paused to look at him.

'I'll need my quilt,' he said. 'And my pillow and my bedside light. I wonder what Mum's doing.'

'I'll go and spy on her when I wake up,' offered Henry. 'I'm very good at spying.'

'OK,' said Charlie, still busy with the tin-opener.

Henry snored a few more snores and then said, 'Charlie, do you think it might get quite boring, living behind this shed?'

111

'No,' said Charlie.

'I'm bored *now*!'

Charlie grunted.

'I think I'll go and start spying.'

'Go on then.'

Henry crawled out from behind the shed again, across the garden, and crept silently up to the kitchen window.

'Hello, Henry!' said Charlie's mother, popping open the door so unexpectedly that Henry fell over. 'Did you get lonely? Come in, if you like. I'm on the phone. To a computer helpline. In a queue. What can I do for you?'

'I was just wondering ...'

'Mmmm?'

'Now that Charlie's run away ...'

'Yes, yes? Hurry up! I am moving up

the queue.'

'... if you would mind me using his stuff?'

'Using it?'

'Taking it.'

'Goodness, no!' said Charlie's mother cheerfully. 'Help yourself! We shan't be needing it again, I don't suppose ... Hello, hello? Oh wonderful! A human voice at last!'

She waved Henry away and hurried into the front room with the phone. Henry, feeling deliciously like a burglar, rushed upstairs to Charlie's bedroom.

'Help yourself!' Charlie's mother had said. Henry did. He found Charlie's quilt, pillow, slippers and pyjamas and flung them out of the window to land

on the lawn
below. Next he
unplugged the
bedside lamp
and lowered
it down by the
flex on to the quilt.
Finally, he staggered down
the stairs with Charlie's bedside table.

It took him less than five minutes.
Charlie's mother did not see a thing.

'Brilliant!' said Charlie, when all these
things appeared behind the shed. 'Didn't
she mind?'

'She said I could,' said Henry. 'She
said she wouldn't be needing it again.
She's still trying to get that computer
fixed. Crikey! Did you make that great

big hole just with a tin-opener?'

'It's good, isn't it?' asked Charlie, and he looked proudly at the results of his work, a jagged hole, easily big enough to get a hand through.

'What's it for?'

'There's plugs in that shed, Henry,' said Charlie mysteriously.

'Sink plugs?'

'Electric plugs,' said Charlie, 'and I can reach them.'

By the end of the afternoon Henry's burglaring and Charlie's hole had changed everything. Now the carpet was down and the bed was made. The bedside lamp was glowing and the PlayStation and TV were unpacked and

115

set up. Charlie and Henry (eating hot pizza, chips and salad absent-mindedly made by Charlie's mother and dumped on the lawn for the cat) were squabbling over the controls.

'I should have run away ages ago,' said Charlie.

Henry shared the last chip fairly in half and asked, 'What'll you do when I've gone?'

'Gone? Gone where?'

'Home,' said Henry.

'Are you going home?'

'*I* haven't run away,' Henry reminded him.

Charlie suddenly didn't want his last half chip. All at once, life behind the shed seemed much less cosy. Still he said bravely, 'I expect I'll stay up all night. I've always wanted to. When are you going, so I can get started?'

'Now,' said Henry.

'*Now?*'

'Yes,' said Henry, and went.

Gone for Hours

After Henry had gone there followed a time when Charlie became so bored his stomach ached and he thought he must be ill.

Suddenly there were footsteps in the garden: Max, pushing his bike round the corner of the house.

'Hi, Max!' he heard his mother call. 'Did you have a good time?'

'Yes, thanks,' said Max.

'Supper very soon, when Dad comes home.  Just the three of us, because Charlie's run away.'

'He has?' asked Max. 'Oh superb! Fantastic! At last!'

Behind the shed Charlie pulled awful faces at Max. He was still pulling them when his father came home.

This time both Max and his mother rushed out to tell the news.

'Charlie's run away!' they said happily. 'It's been so peaceful.

119

We can't imagine where he's gone but he's definitely completely vanished!'

Charlie's father had already heard what had happened to the computer, and had just been stopped by the owner of number sixty-two and shown the remains of the fence. So he was not in a good mood. He said it should not be hard to find Charlie.

'Just a matter of following the trail of destruction he leaves everywhere he goes!' he said.

'No, no,' said Charlie's mother. 'You do not understand! He's been gone for hours; he must be miles away by now. Poor Henry has had to play on his own here all afternoon.'

'Henry's not run away too, then?'

asked Charlie's father in a hopeful kind of voice.

'Oh no,' said Charlie's mother. 'Henry would not have to do that. Charlie told me this morning that Henry is far better looked after than he is. He does not have a horrible rotten mother always fussing. Or a bossy big brother or a father who never shares his stuff. I am terribly sorry about the computer. I had only turned my back for a minute to get the parachute off the cat ... Charlie made her a parachute, you see, very early this morning, before he got up. Poor old Suzy!'

I was being kind! thought Charlie, listening indignantly. I was *helping* her! She was sitting very dangerously on the

banister without a parachute!

'So that's what happened to my football shirt!' grumbled Max. 'I wondered why it was all tied up with bits of string.'

It was an emergency! thought Charlie. Which is most important, your football shirt or our faithful only cat?

'Poor old Max,' Charlie heard his father say as they all went inside.

Poor old Max now! thought Charlie, all alone again. What about poor old Charlie! Having to live out here behind the shed! All by myself! In the dark! In the …

Something cold hit Charlie on the face.

'RAIN!' exclaimed Charlie.

It was true it was raining. Slow, heavy drops were falling on Charlie, and Charlie's bed and bedside lamp, and worst of all, on Charlie's portable TV and PlayStation.

'Oh!' thought Charlie, frantically unplugging and stuffing and packing. 'What shall I do?'

He had two choices, he realized.

He could either go home and put up with his awful family, or he would go somewhere further away. Somewhere dry and comfy.

By the time he had his bags packed his mind was made up. He pushed the Thomas rug and beanbag into the shed, picked up his backpack and his impossibly heavy bags, draped his quilt over his shoulders like a cloak and headed off down the road to Henry's house.

Luckily, Henry's back door was open and there was no one in the kitchen. From the living room came the sound of the TV and of Henry's mother talking on the phone. Charlie crept up the stairs and past the bathroom. Henry's

bedroom was empty too, but from the
bathroom came terrific splashing and
Henry's voice ordering, 'Dive, dive,
dive!' Silently Charlie lowered his bags
to the floor, and flopped down on
Henry's bed.

Henry was very surprised
to find that Charlie
had run away to his
house, but he was
not sorry. He had
felt rather left
out, coming home
alone and leaving all the adventures to
Charlie. So he willingly helped Charlie
hide his belongings in the cupboard,
fetched him the biscuit tin and went
downstairs to ask for two mugs of hot

chocolate instead of one.

'Two?' asked his mother, and she said into the telephone, 'Henry has just come in and asked if he can have two hot chocolates! He must be extra thirsty ...'

Henry put on his extra thirsty face.

'Of course you can,' she said to Henry. 'And two baths if you like, and two pairs of pyjamas ...'

Whoever she was talking to laughed. Henry heard them.

'... but then bed, and no talking ...'

'Talking?' asked Henry, startled.

'... to that hamster ... Shall I come and tuck you up?'

'I will tuck myself up, thank you,' said Henry angelically, 'to save you bothering.'

Charlie stayed hidden
at Henry's house for
thirty-nine hours. He
knew it was that long,
because he counted.

It was a time of
great quietness.

Food was the easy part. Henry was
always appearing with piles of the stuff.
Henry's mother seemed to leave it lying
around in uncounted heaps: bunches of
bananas, sausage rolls, cartons of fruit
juice, boxes of cereal, cheese sticks and
sandwiches.

'I should like toast,' said Charlie.

Henry brought toast but it was not
like home toast. It was made with the
wrong sort of bread and spread with

the wrong sort of butter. It did not smell right, either.

'You're too fussy,' said Henry crossly, when Charlie complained. 'You'd better eat as much as you can, whether you like it or not. I might not be able to get any more for ages.'

Henry said this with everything he brought. He made it sound like starvation might happen any moment. Charlie ate until he was stuffed and ungrateful. When Henry appeared on Friday afternoon with a plateful of warm-out-of-the-oven chocolate cakes, Charlie pushed them out of sight under the bed. All that night he could smell them there, and it made him feel awful.

The nights were very long. Charlie

slept on Henry's floor, with Henry's sleeping bag underneath him, and his own quilt on top. It was not like a sleepover because they could not talk. It was as uninteresting as going to bed at home, except that instead of Max telling ghost stories for company, he had Henry snoring and muttering and tossing the bedclothes about.

But the days were worse than the nights.

During the day Henry and Charlie played silently with every game that Henry owned. They made models out of every piece of Lego. They fitted together every jigsaw puzzle.

It was terribly boring for Charlie, but it was all right for Henry. When he grew tired of the silent bedroom life he could escape. He could tear round the garden kicking goals into his football net. He could watch TV in the living room, or scrape out a cake bowl in the kitchen.

Best of all, he could be noisy. He could jump down the stairs with enormous crashes. He could ring his bike bell or chatter to the man mending the fence at number sixty-two, or yell across the garden to Lulu. Charlie, listening to these happy sounds, felt more and more like a prisoner.

'Not a prisoner!' said

Henry, insulted, when Charlie told him this. 'More like a ... like a ... like a pet! Like Hammy!'

Hammy was Henry's hamster. He also lived in Henry's bedroom, constantly supplied with delicious food and terrible toys. He also kept his extra supplies under the bed.

Sometimes Hammy bit people.

Charlie could understand why.

No Charlie

Charlie could never have survived the thirty-nine hours in Henry's bedroom if it wasn't for one thing.

His family.

After Charlie ran away, Charlie's family took to visiting Henry's family very often. They seemed to need to talk about Charlie. They would sit in the garden under Henry's bedroom window and talk and talk. Charlie could hear every word.

At first their visits were quite cheerful. They talked in loud cheerful voices about what a good time they were having without Charlie, and what an even better time he must be having without them.

But by Friday afternoon, when Charlie had been gone for a whole day and a night, things were changing.

Charlie's dad started it. He began to complain. He complained about the quietness at home.

'Quiet makes me jumpy,' he said. 'Max is never any good at being properly noisy. Not, you know, *totally* noisy. I don't know why, but he can never seem to manage it … We miss Charlie, for noise.'

This pleased Charlie very much, and he could understand it too. Quietness had never been his favourite thing, and lately it had begun to drive him mad.

The next person to complain was Max. Max said he was bored, and this must have been true because it took hardly any persuading to get him to be a goalie for Henry.

Max stopped twenty goals in a row, the last five with his hands behind his back to prove how useless Henry was at football.

Henry said no wonder Charlie had run away.

'What do you know about Charlie

running away?' asked Max.

'I know a lot,' said Henry, looking at
Max with sinister half-closed eyes to pay
him back for stopping all his goals.

'Do you think he'll ever come back?'

'Nope!'

'I bet he's getting pretty hungry by
now.'

'I bet he isn't,' said Henry.

'Cold too, at night.'

'Boiling hot,' said Henry firmly.

'It's not much fun at home without
him. Mum and Dad have no one to

moan at except me.'

'You'll get used to it,' said Henry. 'It's my turn in goal. Come on.'

So Max shot twenty goals past Henry, the last three with his eyes shut, and Henry said he wasn't playing any more.

'Were you watching?' he asked Charlie in bed that night. 'Did you see how hard your rotten brother kicked that ball?'

'Much less hard than usual,' said

Charlie. 'He was hardly trying.'

'What's he like when he tries, then?'

'Fantastic. Do you think he's missing me?'

'No.'

'Not even a bit?'

'No.'

'I think,' said Charlie, 'he's missing me a lot.'

'Henry and Hammy!' called Henry's mother up the stairs. 'Shush now!'

So they shushed, and Charlie soon fell asleep, tired out with doing nothing. He woke on Saturday morning to the sound of Max's voice, calling up under the bedroom window.

'Henry!'

'What?' asked Henry. 'What? What is it?

Oh, Max! What d'you want?'

'Tell Charlie there's a great big parcel just come for him at our house!'

'All right,' said Henry. 'I'll tell him …'

'Ha!' said Max, sounding extremely pleased.

'… if I ever see him again!'

Max stamped home, defeated, and later Charlie sent Henry to collect his parcel.

'How?' asked Henry.

'Just ask,' Charlie said. 'They'll let you have it. They let you have my other stuff, didn't they?'

Charlie was right. They did let Henry have it. He returned to Charlie in triumph and Charlie tore off the wrappers and found a double-barrelled

138

supersonic water-squirter, the perfect
present from his Uncle Pete, exactly
what he had been wanting all summer.

'I need to try it out!' he said.

'Where?'

Charlie looked around. It was true
that upstairs in someone else's bedroom
was not the place to test a double-
barrelled water-squirter.

'Out the window,' he said
at last.

'You can't,'
said Henry.
'Your mum's
out there.
Grumbling
to my mum.
About toast.'

'Toast?' asked Charlie, suddenly interested. 'Toast!' And he crept to the window to listen.

'... so much in the habit,' he heard. 'I've got so much in the habit of making stacks of toast for Charlie that I can't seem to stop! I've done it again this morning! The bird table's piled high. The cat won't touch it. I just can't get used to him being gone ...'

She sounded so sad that Charlie could hardly bear it.

'I should write myself a reminder and stick it on the toaster ...'

Charlie's eyes prickled with tears.

'... saying NO CHARLIE ...'

Charlie could endure it no more. It wasn't having a water-squirter and

NO CHARLIE

nowhere to squirt it. It wasn't because
Max was missing him so much he had
to play football with Henry. It wasn't
the quietness that made his father
jumpy.

It was the thought of that label on the
toaster.

He pushed past Henry and ran down
the stairs, through the door, past his
amazed mother, out of the garden

and along the street and into his own familiar kitchen. And by the time Henry caught up with him, it was like a party in there. A toast party, with a water fight afterwards, Charlie and Henry against Max and Lulu and Mellie, with the dads joining in, and the mothers hugging each other, and everyone saying, 'Oh, isn't it wonderful! Charlie's come home!'

'I never ran away myself,' remarked Max, when he and Charlie were finally in bed that night. 'What's it like?'

'Fantastic,' said Charlie.

'What's the best bit?'

'Oh,' said Charlie. 'The last bit, I think. Coming home. And everyone

being sorry. And then forgiving them
all. Like a hero ...'

Max smiled in the dark.

'... like me!' said Charlie.

WANT MORE CHARLIE?
READ MORE OF HIS ADVENTURES

in
CHARLIE
and the Tooth Fairy

The First Tooth

Charlie had four wobbly teeth.
He had:

One that was rather wobbly.

One that was quite wobbly.

One that was slightly wobbly.

One that was

just beginning to be wobbly.

He had them all together, and he was very excited about it because they were his first wobbly teeth.

Charlie also had a big brother called Max. Max was very clever. He knew things most other people didn't know, like what chewing gum was made of and how magnets worked and the way to tell if strange dogs were friendly or not. Max knew so much and was right so often that it was hardly worth arguing with him.

Whenever Charlie wanted to know something he would go to Max for the answer. And if he wanted to prove to anyone that something was true he would say, 'If you don't believe me, ask Max!'

And then whoever Charlie was talking to would know that it really was true, because everyone knew how clever Max was.

So Max was a very useful brother to Charlie.

But Max was not useful when Charlie discovered that he had four wobbly teeth.

Charlie showed Max his wobbliest tooth, and asked, 'How can I make it come out faster?'

Max looked at the tooth and said, 'You can't. It's not that loose! It might be there for ages yet! Anyway, what's the hurry?'

'I need it for the tooth fairy,' said

Charlie, with his fingers in his mouth,
giving his wobbliest tooth an extra
wobble. Charlie was very much looking
forward to getting his teeth out, one by
one, and leaving them under his pillow
for the tooth fairy. His best friend,
Henry, had told him about her.

'The tooth fairy!' repeated Max. 'The
tooth fairy is for kids!'

'For kids?'

'Yes, *and*,' said Max, 'the tooth fairy is a waste of teeth!'

'A waste of teeth?'

'You'll find out!' said Max, walking away.

After Max had gone, Charlie remembered that his brother had always been like this about the tooth fairy. When Max's own teeth had fallen out he had not put them under his pillow. He had hidden them away in a secret place instead.

'Who wants fairies crawling around their bed while they're asleep?' Max had asked. 'And what kind of person sells *their own teeth*?'

Max was no help at all about wobbly teeth, but Charlie's best friend, Henry, was.

Henry was an expert on teeth. Four of his had come out already. He didn't care. He liked the gaps. He had pulled all four out himself, and enjoyed doing it. He thought he might be a dentist one day, just for the pleasure of pulling out teeth.

When Charlie's wobbliest tooth refused to get any more wobbly and it began to look like it really

wouldn't be out for ages (just like Max had said), Henry kindly offered to help speed it up.

'If you're really sure you want it out,' he said.

'Of course I am!'

'Well then,' said Henry. 'You need a method. In fact, you need *The Newly Invented Look At The Lovely View Method.*'

'Do I?'

'Trust me, I'm an expert,' said Henry, and Charlie, who knew that in the matter of teeth Henry really was an expert, said, 'OK.'

Then Henry went home and returned with a reel of dental floss.

It takes a monster
to know a monster!

MONSTER ✚ HOSPITAL

THE BIG FAT SMELLY OGRE
GILLIAN JOHNSON

THE DISASTROUS LITTLE DRAGON
GILLIAN JOHNSON

THE YUCKY YODELLING YETI
GILLIAN JOHNSON

Join grumpy Sylvie, bossy Carolyn, clever-clogs Tom and disgusting Dylan, the most monstrous children in school, as they are tasked with curing monsters of mysterious and revolting illnesses.

Also available
as an ebook

www.hodderchildrens.co.uk

Hodder
Children's
Books

Neal Layton's classic, lovable mammoths, Oscar and Arabella, are off to school and there's always trouble around the corner at The Mammoth Academy!